CUAA926025

Breeze of Love

Breeze of Love

A Romantic Drama

Nicholas Vern

PALMETTO
PUBLISHING
Charleston, SC
www.PalmettoPublishing.com

Breeze of Love
Copyright © 2023 by Nicholas Vern

All rights reserved

No portion of this book may be reproduced, stored in a retrieval system, or transmitted in any form by any means—electronic, mechanical, photocopy, recording, or other—except for brief quotations in printed reviews, without prior permission of the author.

Hardcover ISBN: 979-8-8229-2054-5
Paperback ISBN: 979-8-8229-2055-2

Cast Of Characters

Big Daddy is an older gentleman, who is the master of ceremonies of the circus. He's husky, distinguished gentleman in his Eighties.

George is a heavyset, amateur clown who loves the circus.

Nicholas is a handsome, kind, young architect.

Elaina is a beautiful, young acrobat (late twenties) with blue eyes, fair skin, and blond hair.

Pierre is muscular, harsh-looking acrobat (late thirties).

Mother and Father (Nicholas' parents) are a neat-looking, aristocratic couple.

Little Nicholas is Elaina's and Nicholas's son.

This play takes place in the early 1950s.

Breeze Of Love

FADE IN:

INT. CIRCUS BIG TOP – DAY

There is a lot of tension under the big tent of the famous Tripolink Circus. A set-up crew, along with performers, is working hard under the supervision of a big, older gentleman (Big Daddy) in order to finish on time.

There are only about thirty minutes left before the opening of the first performance of the season.

Big Daddy calls for everybody to get involved and help.

BIG DADDY

(he yells)

We are falling behind. You only have twenty minutes to finish. Let's move faster!

He urges those who work up above, setting up for the acrobats, to finish up in a hurry.

BIG DADDY

Come on, you guys. Hurry up and finish.

He is nervous. He yells at some jugglers for choosing the wrong time to practice.

BIG DADDY

Hey you! Get off the stage! Get out of here! And you!

He chases a midget around the stage for not helping. Not being able to catch him, he threatens him.

BIG DADDY

(continuing)

You little shit, if I catch you,
I will shrink you down to nothing.

INT. SOMEWHERE IN THE CITY, IN AN APARTMENT ROOM – DAY

In a room, in front of a mirror, a heavy set clown (George) is making up his face, making faces, and talking to himself as if he were talking to the audience.

GEORGE

And now, ladies and gentlemen, I present to you the greatest clown on earth,

(in a lower voice)

George.

He laughs and applauds for himself. The door opens, and a handsome young man holding a briefcase enters the room. George welcomes him.

GEORGE

Here comes Nicholas, the greatest architect of all. He is going to redesign the Parthenon one of these days.

Nicholas looks at him and walks to the connected room with a kind smile, shaking his head.

George is following him. He leaves his briefcase next to a desk, piled up with papers and books.

George follows him, clowning around.

GEORGE

(practicing with a deck of cards)

Here you see the fifty-two cards. Pick up a card, young man.

(pretends that a card was picked up and shuffles the cards, then asks)

Is this the number you picked?

Nicholas pays little attention to George, who is proudly trying to perform a trick (the raw egg between his fingers didn't work out, and instead of the egg disappearing, it falls on the floor).

GEORGE

(upset, pulls a rag out of his pocket, bends down, cleans, and talks as he cleans)

You rotten egg!

NICHOLAS

Okay, okay, now tell me what is going on.

GEORGE

(his voice changes, and in a serious tone, he replies)

Nicholas, tonight is the night. Tonight, my dear friend, is the grand opening of the greatest circus in the world, the famous Tripolink Circus. And your good friend George is going to be performing.

(getting down on his knees, like begging)

Would you please come tonight to admire your best friend, your buddy, and your roommate performing?

(he pulls out a lollipop)

Please, Nicholas, you have to come; I need you.

NICHOLAS

(walks away, saying)

I would love to come, George, but I am piled up with work, and tomorrow I have a big presentation.

GEORGE

Please, Nicholas. I beg you.

At the end, George convinces him to go along. He pulls a ticket from his pocket with a smile.

GEORGE

This, my friend, will get you to the third row, center seat.

INT. BIG TOP - EVENING

The flap doors of the circus tent are open. Nicholas is welcomed by George, who is anxiously waiting for him, and directs him to his seat.

George, by the main entrance, is directing everybody who needs help to find their seats. Sometimes playing tricks on the innocent spectators who need help finding their seats, he takes them around different sections pretending he is looking for their seats, and has them follow him all over the place.

Proudly, he looks at Nicholas, making a point to hang around in the section where Nicholas is seated.

George blows up some balloons for the kids.

At some point, knowing that he is being watched, he attempts the egg trick. Nicholas covers his eyes, and he uncovers them only when he hears applause around him. George proudly makes the thumbs-up sign at Nicholas.

All the seats are full at the circus. The time comes for the sound of the trumpet announcing the beginning of the show. Spotlights light up the stage as the band plays a marching tune and the show begins.

Big Daddy, in his formal, colorful tuxedo suit, announces and introduces the performers as they are marching around the ring in the rhythm of the sounds of the band.

Nicholas's eyes get stuck on this young, agile, and beautiful performer. She is riding while standing up on the back of a horse. Her arms open, smiling and throwing kisses, she bows to the applauding crowd.

NICHOLAS

(to himself)

God, she is beautiful.

He is applauding with excitement, as are all members of the audience.

The show begins with the performance of the trained, performing dogs doing tricks, followed by clowns, magicians, jugglers, etc.

Then, everything goes silent. Big Daddy comes out on stage.

BIG DADDY

The next performer I am about to introduce is the well-known, magnificent, and unbelievable acrobatic duo. Ladies and gentlemen, I am proud to introduce the magnificent Elaina and Pierre.

People are applauding enthusiastically.

Pierre is a strong, harsh-looking man in his early forties.

She is a beautiful young lady in her upper twenties. She has blond hair, fair skin, and beautiful blue eyes. She is petite and looks even smaller standing next to Pierre.

She is the one Nicholas had noticed from the beginning, and now he is watching her closely, applauding as she bows to the audience and heads over, with Pierre, to the two hanging ropes. They start climbing in the same rhythm to the top. When they get there, they stand next to each other on the elevated platform, and they salute the audience again.

The audience replies to their salute with a lot of applause and noise. The band starts playing. Pierre grabs the horizontal bar in front of him and swings smoothly back and forth. Elaina does the same.

They perform different impressive and dangerous acts. There is no net below.

The crowd applauds at the end of each act. Then Big Daddy (the master of ceremonies) comes to the center of the stage and asks:

BIG DADDY

Now, ladies and gentlemen, I would like to ask for your complete silence. You are about to see the most dangerous act ever performed in a circus by anyone without a protective net. It is a matter of life or death! Please stay calm and quiet.

The drums sound, and the two acrobats get ready for their big act. Pierre swings first, hanging from the horizontal bar. Then he switches positions, hanging down with his knees locked over the horizontal bar.

He swings back and forth in a precise rhythm, anticipating Elaina performing her act.

IN SLOW MOTION

Elaina releases her hands from the bar as she is swinging in the air. First flip, second flip, and then at the critical instant, she is grabbed and saved by Pierre's powerful hands.

The audience applauds hysterically as the two acrobats slide down their ropes. When they reach the ground, Elaina and Pierre continue to bow and blow kisses to the audience.

There is a standing ovation.

Nicholas, along with the crowd, continues to applaud, and he is standing up even after everyone else has been seated.

NICHOLAS

(to an older lady sitting next to him)

Isn't she beautiful? Isn't she gorgeous?

The old lady looks at him kind of funny and moves herself farther away from him.

As soon as the show is over, feeling proud and looking for a compliment, George goes toward Nicholas.

NICHOLAS

(seems to be in a different world)

(MORE)

NICHOLAS (cont'd)

George.

GEORGE

Well, Nicholas. Wasn't it a great show? And your buddy?

(assuming Nicholas is going to pay a compliment to him.)

What do you have to say about this?

NICHOLAS

I'm telling you buddy, you were great. But that gorgeous blonde acrobat—oh man, she is the most beautiful girl I have ever seen in my life. I'd love to meet her. George, I *have* to meet her. You understand?

GEORGE

To meet whom? That beautiful blonde acrobat?

NICHOLAS

Yes, George. How can I do this? How can I meet her?

GEORGE

(George pretends he is thinking and touches his cheek with his index
finger, whispering)

Oh, you mean, Elaina? That beautiful, gorgeous
blonde acrobat? I think it can be done. Come on, I
know where she lives. Let's go and find her.

Nicholas smiles from ear to ear and follows his friend, who leads him
to a section of the trailers where all the performers live. He stops in
front of one of them.

GEORGE

Here it is.

Nicholas stands behind, kind of shy, while George climbs up the two
steps of the trailer, places his face on the glass window at the upper
part of the door, and looks inside.

Elaina is sitting in front of her mirror, removing the makeup from
her face. Realizing that someone is looking at her, she gets up and
comes to the door. George steps down as she opens the door.

ELAINA

(politely)

Hi! Is there something I can do for you?

GEORGE

No. Not for me, but for my friend here.

(points to Nicholas, who stands behind him, scared, with his head down)

He is dying to meet you.

(he nods his head up and down, as if to assure Elaina)

ELAINA

Oh, hello!

NICHOLAS

Hello!

ELAINA

Did you enjoy the show?

NICHOLAS

Very much indeed, and you are so beautiful. You are magnificent.

ELAINA

Oh, thank you! You're so kind.

(she walks down the steps)

ELAINA

My name is Elaina. What's yours?

NICHOLAS

Nicholas. So nice to meet you.

ELAINA

So nice to meet you, too, Nicholas.

(she looks at him)

ELAINA

(continuing)

You are a handsome young man.

NICHOLAS

Thank you. Sorry to come here empty-handed. Such a beautiful performance. I wish I had some flowers to offer you, but...

ELAINA

Oh, don't worry about that.

NICHOLAS

I'm very happy to be meeting you.

GEORGE

(repeating after Nicholas)

He is very, very happy.

He stops when Nicholas gives him a dirty look, raises his arms, not knowing what to do or how to react, and turns around to walk away.

Nicholas, while taking a few steps backward.

NICHOLAS

It is so nice meeting you, Elaina.

(Nicholas turns to follow his friend George)

ELAINA

Don't leave. Would you stay? I'll be ready in a minute! I'm almost done.

As a matter of fact, I am finished. I will show you around if you wish.

NICHOLAS

(smiles at her with a sweet and satisfied smile; he looks around for
George, who has already left; he looks at Elaina, smiling)

Sure, I'd love to.

The two are walking together to the compound. She takes him to
the areas where the elephants are kept. Some of the trainers are still
around. Elaina says hello to them. She shows him the cage with the
tigers.

ELAINA

Oh! They are mean.

She holds his hand and leads him to another cage where a bunch of
little monkeys are staying. She goes close to the cage. The monkeys
come by the bars; they jump up and down in happiness when they
see Elaina. She pats them while talking to them.

ELAINA

I have no bananas for you. Sorry, guys.

(to Nicholas)

They are my friends. I love them.

Farther down, they meet the old gentleman who announces the
show, walking toward his trailer.

Elaina runs to him, calling him, "Big Daddy." He stops and opens
his arms. They hug each other.

Big Daddy gives her a kiss on top of her head.

ELAINA

Big Daddy, I want you to meet my friend, Nicholas.

They shake hands.

NICHOLAS

Nice meeting you.

(lowering his voice)

Big Daddy.

BIG DADDY

Nice to meet you, young man.

Elaina gives him a kiss and then walks away with Nicholas while they say good night to Big Daddy.

BIG DADDY

Elaina, be careful.

ELAINA

(answering)

Always, Big Daddy. Always.

ELAINA

(to Nicholas)

He always tells me to be careful. Big Daddy and the little monkeys you met are the only true friends I have.

NICHOLAS

Your parents?

ELAINA

I never met my parents. Big Daddy and his wife brought me up before she passed away. My mother, I was told, passed away when I was born.

They remain silent as they walk away. Nicholas holds her hand. His face shows sympathy and kindness.

They walk back outside to her trailer. They turn and look at each other. They stand there holding hands for quite some time, but neither one shows any desire to leave.

Elaina takes his hands, raises them up, puts them on her cheeks, and looks at him.

ELAINA

It was wonderful meeting you. I hope to see you again very soon.

(she whispers)

Good night.

NICHOLAS

(watching her walk up the steps)

Good night. Great meeting you, too.

(whispering)

Can I call you?

ELAINA

(stopping for a moment before entering her trailer)

Please do. I'd love to hear from you again.

Nicholas walks toward the exit of the complex, feeling as if he is in a different world from when he arrived at the circus. He is full of happiness and sweet thoughts. He is walking, not really knowing exactly where he is going.

The sound of a car horn stops him. His friend George is waiting for him. Nicholas gets into the car, sits straight up, and holds his head with his hands. He is dreaming and not talking. They drive away silently.

George looks at him from time to time, wondering if he is okay. Finally, he turns to Nicholas.

GEORGE

Well, did you enjoy the show? Was it worth it?

NICHOLAS

(shakes his head slowly up and down a few times)

Oh yes!

It was excellent, and you were magnificent. Thank
you. Thank you, George.

George smiles with satisfaction, and with a big smile on his face, he
drives toward their house.

INT. APARTMENT - NIGHT

They are entering the apartment they share.

GEORGE

Good night.

George enters his room.

Nicholas goes to his own room, takes off his jacket, sits at his desk,
turns on the desk lamp, and leans forward, holding his head.

NICHOLAS

(whispers to himself)

What an evening.

Nicholas turns around toward the door that connects to George's
room.

NICHOLAS

Hey, George! George.

GEORGE

Yes, Nicholas.

NICHOLAS

She asked me to call her, but I don't know her
number. George, help me, please.

GEORGE

Hmm. A magician has to work hard for this,
Nicholas. It's a hard trick to perform, my friend. Let
me see. Let me get to my card deck and see what I can
do.

(He takes his deck out of his pocket and goes behind the door. He
shuffles the cards, holding them upside down. He pulls one out
without looking at it and shoves it under Nicholas's bedroom door.)

Nicholas pays no attention to the card.

George walks to his desk and opens his telephone directory. He takes
out a blank card and writes a number on it, while at the same time,
on another blank card, he copies another number from his telephone
directory.

GEORGE

(to Nicholas)

Look at it. Look at this card. Is this the same number
as the first one?

NICHOLAS

Come on, George. This is not the time for games.

GEORGE

(insisting)

Pick up a card.

Nicholas picks up the cards and turns them over.

NICHOLAS

No, George. They don't match.

GEORGE

Damn it.

(he shoves the other card under the door)

GEORGE

How about this?

Nicholas, with regret, picks up the second card. A telephone number and the name Elaina are written on it.

NICHOLAS

You son of a gun. George, you are a true magician.

GEORGE

(with a smile, indicating his satisfaction)

That's me, all right. Good luck.

NICHOLAS

Good night, George. And thanks!

(he is holding the card with Elaina's number on it and looking at it)

Oh, my God. What's happening to me? I am falling in love. I'm in love.

I don't feel comfortable calling her.

(MORE)

NICHOLAS (cont'd)

I should send her flowers and a card. No, no. I should write her a letter.

(he takes a pen and starts writing, speaking his thoughts out loud as he writes them to her)

Dear Elaina,

I want to thank you for your kindness. It was the most wonderful evening I've ever had.

You are not only beautiful, but you are also a wonderful person.

I cannot stop thinking of you, which is why I decided to write this letter and tell you.

He stops writing.

NICHOLAS

(to himself)

No, no. I should call her.

No, it's too late.

(looks at his watch)

It is past midnight. It's too late, too late to call her.

He pauses; he is thinking, and suddenly, not able to resist any longer, he picks up the phone and dials her number.

Elaina picks up the phone on the first ring.

Nicholas is nervous; he starts talking to her by reading the letter he wrote to her.

NICHOLAS

Dear Elaina,

I want to thank you for your kindness. It was the most wonderful evening I've ever had.

(MORE)

NICHOLAS (cont'd)

You are not only beautiful but also a wonderful person. I cannot stop thinking of you, which is why I decided to write this letter.

(he realizes his mistake and corrects himself)

I mean, that's why I decided to call you. I hope you don't mind for…

ELAINA

I am so happy you called. I couldn't sleep either.

(with embarrassment)

Thinking of you.

(shy)

You are so nice, so kind, and different from the people I know.

There is silence for a while, then.

NICHOLAS

I want to see you soon, I need to see you soon, very soon, like tomorrow!

ELAINA

I would love to see you, too. Tomorrow is an early show. I will be free at 3:00 p.m.

NICHOLAS

I will be waiting by your front door at 3:00 p.m.

ELAINA

No. Wait for me by the front entrance.

NICHOLAS

Great. I'll be there. Good night, and Elaina, be careful.

ELAINA

(smiling)

I will. Good night.

They hang up.

EXT. - CIRCUS - EVENING

The show is over, and Nicholas is by the entrance, standing in front of his car, waiting, and holding a bouquet of flowers. People are walking around him, leaving after the show. Nicholas is nervous; he is anxious to see Elaina. He's search his eyes among the crowd.

Finally, she appears, looking around for him.

Nicholas walks over to her, hands her the flowers, and together they walk to his car. He opens the door for her. Elaina looks around, hoping not to be seen by any of the circus people. He closes her door, goes around the car, jumps in the driver's seat, and they drive away.

They drive through a country road with tall trees on either side and wild flowers all over.

ELAINA

What beautiful scenery!

A gentle breeze is blowing through the open window, as is the soft fragrance of the flowers. Elaina takes a deep breath.

ELAINA

It's so nice, Nicholas. It is so nice.

(she takes his hand into her hands)

The road took them up a hill. A spectacular view was extended in front of them. He stops the car. They move close together, inspired by the scenery. Nicholas places his arms around her, both looking fascinated without saying a word, looking at a lake far away from them and a small, photographic village.

ELAINA

So picturesque. Isn't it wonderful?

NICHOLAS

That sparkling lake is called Geneva Lake.

And there, by the water, is my family's summer home—right in front of the water. I love that place. I could live there year-round. I would like to take you there sometime.

Elaina puts her hands around his neck, looking at him.

ELAINA

I would love to go.

Nicholas gives her a kiss on the cheek. Elaina comes closer, and they kiss each other.

NICHOLAS

I am in love with you. I loved you as soon as I saw you. You are beautiful.

ELAINA

And you are so different, so nice, and so gentle.

It's rough in the circus; it's a rough world, but this is the only world I know. I always dreamed of the outside world as a garden, a paradise full of flowers and nice people. Something like this.

(points outside toward the beautiful scenery)

But I guess it gets ugly out there, they say.

(she looks at her watch)

Oh my! It's 7:30 p.m. I cannot believe the time went by so fast. I have to get back.

They drive back to the compound. They kiss each other. He leaves her outside.

NICHOLAS

I love you with all my heart.

She walks toward the entrance, turns around, and waves to him. She is happy. On the way to the trailer, there are kids running and shouting hello to her. She replies with a wave. Someone is walking with an elephant and waves to her.

Two jugglers are practicing. She runs between them, interrupting their act. Bottles are falling down.

JUGGLERS

You little bitch!

(they chase her away)

She runs toward her trailer, still happy.

In front of her door, Pierre is waiting for her. He looks mean. He stops her, grabbing her arm as she tries to step up.

PIERRE

Where have you been?

ELAINA

Outside.

PIERRE

Outside? With whom?

ELAINA

With someone I like.

PIERRE

(angry)

Is that so? You don't need to. You belong here. Put that in your mind.

Those outsiders. They come and go, and they bring disaster as they disappear.

(MORE)

PIERRE

Stop it, you hear? Stop it! If not, I'll stop you.

ELAINA

It's not your business. It is about me. My life! Not
yours, you hear? Leave me alone!

(she pushes him aside and opens the door to her trailer)

PIERRE

(full of irony)

Your life?

(he laughs)

Just don't forget that your life is also in my hands.

(walks away repeating)

In my two hands. Remember it.

Nicholas is there for every performance. He sits in the same seat and
holds a different color flower every time. They meet after the show is
over, and they drive to their special spot.

The first time she invited him back to the circus grounds and inside
her trailer, he noticed a picture of a lady acrobat hanging on the wall.

ELAINA

This is my mother. She was also an acrobat. "A good one," Big Daddy says, "a beautiful woman."

NICHOLAS

Just like you.

(he puts his arms around her)

You look so much like her.

ELAINA

I never met her. She died delivering me.

I talk to her lots of times, apologizing to her. I hope she hears me. She died for me.

(points to a picture of a little girl up on a pony)

And this is me and Big Daddy.

An icon of the Virgin Mary is displayed on a table.

ELAINA

I met a nun once. She came to see the show. I invited her to my trailer, and she talked to me about God and faith.

I have prayed to God every day since then before I go to perform. As a matter of fact, she took this cross off her neck and gave it to me.

(shows Nicholas her cross)

She told me this cross would protect me. I have never taken it off my neck.

I have never been inside a church. I wish I could go one day.

Nicholas keeps visiting her in the trailer often. Sometimes he stays overnight. Pierre is jealous of him and gets furious and ugly. He argues constantly with Elaina about Nicholas.

During one of their visits, while lying in bed, Nicholas opens up and shares his thoughts with her.

NICHOLAS

You are magnificent! Your act is breathtaking. When you are about to jump, everybody wonders what is going to happen. Will Pierre catch you?

(MORE)

NICHOLAS

Or will they witness your beautiful body falling down to your death?

I am worried about you, Elaina! I am worrying all the time! I love you so much! I don't want to see you perform this life-threatening, dangerous act.

Please come with me. Walk away from this deadly act. Let's go and have a different life. We cannot live like this anymore.

Let's get married. We'll have children. We can live in my parent's house by the water, go fishing, and watch the boats go by.

We can buy our own boat and sail, feeling the lovely breeze—a breeze of love with you and me!

She puts her head on his chest. They stay there without saying a word.

INT. CIRCUS TENT - EVENING

The show has started with the ponies performing, etc.

Behind the stage, Elaina and Pierre are getting ready to perform by doing their routine stretching exercises.

Elaina walks toward the curtain. She peeks out, looking where Nicholas usually sits.

Pierre, furious and full of jealousy, walks behind her, looking over her head, and spots Nicholas sitting in his usual seat.

PIERRE

He's there, isn't he?

ELAINA

(turns around, tries to get away and is stopped by his body)

(MORE)

ELAINA (cont'd)

It's none of your business. Stay away.

PIERRE

This guy has to go, you hear me?

ELAINA

Never. Over my dead body. I love him. Is that clear to you?

PIERRE

(sarcastically)

Maybe you will be the dead body!

(as he walks away from her laughing)

ELAINA

You are a sick person. Leave me alone.

BIG DADDY

(out on the stage, announces their act)

Ladies and gentlemen, once again, Elaina and Pierre
will perform for you their magnificent, dangerous
acrobatic act. Please, we need you to be silent. And
remember a small mistake could cause the death of
our dear Elaina.

Elaina and Pierre walk out into the ring.

The audience is welcoming them with their applause. Giving them a
very warm welcome.

Nicholas applauds and stands up.

Elaina responds by looking at him, smiling, and makes a bow.
Pierre's face has a mean look.

They climb up to the landing platform. They wave to the audience
down below.

Pierre looks mean as he starts swinging back and forth, holding the
horizontal bar. There is tension in the air.

Elaina kind of hesitant, goes ahead with their routine. Some jumping
from bar to bar.

People are applauding at the end of each act.

Elaina jumps back to the platform for the ultimate act.

BIG DADDY

(announces)

And now, ladies and gentlemen, I would like to ask
for your complete silence because the next act is very,
very dangerous. A double flip from Elaina in the air.

Her life at this moment is in Pierre's hands to catch her at the right
moment before falling down to her death.

There is tension. Elaina is on the platform and Pierre is swinging
back and forth, looking at her with a strange, mean look, waving her
to go on.

Elaina looks down as if she is looking at Nicholas for the last time.
She is scared. She crosses herself, and grabs the bar and swings, back
and forth.

Pierre, with his legs wrapped around his bar, swings too. His hands
are open, ready for his part.

He claps his hands, one time, signaling her to start her jump. Elaina,
rather nervous, skips the first jump. Pierre looks mad.

He swings again twice. He claps again. Elaina hesitates and does not
respond.

There is a lot of tension down below from the audience as well as the
other performers, watching from the side of the stage.

Pierre comes across for the third time. Elaina (camera in slow
motion) makes her jump. A first flip followed by a second and then

Pierre's powerful hands stop her from falling, but letting purposely one of her hands slip off his hand.

A sound of desperation comes out of Elaina's mouth and the audience's tool

Elaina grabs Pierre's loose hand again and swings up to the platform. He follows her, looks at her sarcastically. They salute the applauding audience. Elaina's face is stiff, without her usual smile. They slide down, they bow to the audience as always. Before the audience stops their applause, Elaina leaves the stage, leaving Pierre behind.

Elaina runs to the back of the stage. There, she picks up her robe from the hanger, and without talking to anybody, she runs out from the side door to her trailer.

Nicholas appears further down the road, walking to her trailer to visit her. She gets in the trailer, locks her door behind her, and breaks into a bad cry.

Nicholas comes to the front door. He looks through the window and sees her crying. He knocks at the door and begs her to open the door. She refuses.

ELAINA

Please leave me alone, please!

Nicholas, convinced that she is not going to let him in, leaves, but as he goes, he makes one last attempt at talking to her.

NICHOLAS

I will wait for you outside. I'll wait for you!

After a while, when she calms down a little, with tears still in her eyes, she runs out of her trailer to Big Daddy's trailer.

Big Daddy is sitting in a reclining chair, reading a paper. There is a bottle of beer and some munchies on the table next to him, which is not a neat sight.

Elaina walks in crying; she sits down on the floor, putting her hands on Big Daddy's knees, and with a breaking voice, she pours her heart out.

ELAINA

Big Daddy. I have to leave. I have to get away from here. Things are getting ugly around here, especially with Pierre. Big Daddy, I have to go!

(she cries harder)

Big Daddy sets aside his paper as she goes on.

ELAINA (cont'd)

I cannot stay here anymore. Please! Praying for my life every day and jumping to my death, hoping that Pierre will catch me. I cannot do it anymore, I can't.

(after a short pause)

You understand me, Big Daddy. You know I'm in love with a nice young man who has talked to me about love. A different kind of love. He is nice, honorable, and gentle. He loves me a lot.

Big Daddy, I love you and the circus, but he wants me to go with him. He wants to give me a life—a different kind of life—to have a future with him.

(with a calmer, sweeter voice)

He wants me to have a family of my own with him. I have to go, Big Daddy!

Big Daddy's eyes are full of tears. He pats her on the head and plays with her hair. He wipes her tears away. He looks at her with empathy, sympathy, and love.

BIG DADDY

Go on.

(after a short pause)

I understand, I understand. Go ahead, with my blessings. I love you. I will always love you.

Elaina looks up at him and kisses his hands.

ELAINA

Thank you, thank you.

(gets up and kisses him, but she is very hesitant as she is getting up)

Good bye, Daddy. Thank you. I love you a lot, too!

Big Daddy stays silent, watching her leave. Tears are running down his face.

BIG DADDY

(his voice breaking with emotion)

Keep in touch, please. You hear?

ELAINA

Yes, yes. I promise, I'll never forget you!

She walks into her trailer, wipes off the makeup from her face, dresses up in a casual outfit, and opens an empty suitcase. She puts in certain of her belongings, including her mother's picture from the wall and her icon. She looks around her place for the last time, and she leaves, heading toward the exit, holding her suitcase and her little bear under her arm.

She says bye to some circus people who are out on her way without stopping. They are looking at her and wondering what she is up to.

She is almost there when at the exit door Pierre appears. Pierre stands by the exit door and walks in front of her.

Pierre is stopping her from going any further.

PIERRE

Where do you think you are going, young lady?

ELAINA

Leave me alone! It's none of your business. I told you that.

(MORE)

ELAINA

(tries to push him aside)

Leave me alone!

(repeats as she is trying to pass through)

Pierre violently grabs her by the arm. He is mad. He drags her back.

PIERRE

(as Elaina is fighting to free herself)

No, you don't. You go no place.

Suddenly, as Pierre is trying to drag her again, for one more time, a big hand from behind grabs his shoulder, and a heavy, serious voice commands him.

LOUD VOICE

Don't! Let her go! Now!

Pierre freezes as he turns his head and sees Big Daddy behind him.

Elaina slips away and runs toward the exit. Nicholas is waiting for her outside his car. He runs to her when he sees her coming. He takes her suitcase and, throws it in the back seat of the car. They both get in the car and drive away, leaving behind the circus and Pierre, mad and yelling.

PIERRE

You will be back! You will be back!

Both happy and relieved, Nicholas and Elaina drive through the road with tall trees on its side to an exclusive neighborhood.

ELAINA

Where are we going?

(looking around at the big houses)

NICHOLAS

To my parent's house.

ELAINA

Do you think they will like me?

NICHOLAS

They will love you.

(he gives her a kiss)

ELAINA

(nervously pulls down the visor and looks at herself in the mirror)

Oh, Nicholas! Look at me. Look at how I look.

NICHOLAS

(looking at her with a smile and admiration)

You look beautiful!

They pull into a circular driveway and stop in front of the door. He comes out of the car, walks up the two granite steps, and rings the bell. Elaina stays in the car, scared. A classy, well-dressed lady opens the door.

NICHOLAS

Hi, Mom.

(they hug and kiss each other)

Nicholas goes back to the car and opens the door for Elaina to get out.

NICHOLAS

Mom, meet Elaina. Elaina gets out of the car.

ELAINA

Hello.

Elaina shakes hands with his mother, who comes down by the car to welcome her.

MOTHER

Come in, dear. Come in.

(she is happy to see them)

What a surprise.

(they enter the large marble foyer)

NICHOLAS

Where's Dad?

MOTHER

Your father is with his animals, as always.

(they both smile)

ELAINA

You have animals here!

NICHOLAS

(confidentially to Elaina)

Dead animals.

MOTHER

(calls)

Dad, Nicholas is here.

FATHER

(voice from inside a room)

Come in, over here.

They open the door to a huge room full of stuffed, mounted animals on the walls as well as the floor.

Father is up on a ladder. A distinguished gray-haired gentleman, wearing a robe jacket, straightened up the head of a wild animal hanging from the wall. He comes down.

NICHOLAS

Hi, Dad!

FATHER

Hi, Son.

(he looks at Elaina)

And who is this beautiful lady with you?

NICHOLAS

This is Elaina, the lady I have been talking about with Mother. We thought we would stop by to say hello.

FATHER

Nice meeting you, Elaina. Come over. Let me show you around.

(Elaina hesitates for a moment and then goes by the father)

This is a zebra. my first hunt on a safari to Kenya.

ELAINA

(looking at the zebra)

My God! She looks alive.

FATHER

This is a rhino. This guy almost got me. As a matter of fact, he threw me up in the air.

I was lucky. I landed behind a tree, and when he turned around, getting ready to charge again, bang, bang. I emptied all my bullets into him.

They keep walking.

And this is a wild cat, fast and dangerous. A mean animal. You better get her with your first shot. Otherwise, you are dead!

ELAINA

(looking around)

You killed all these animals?

NICHOLAS

Of course. Father is a hunter. He loves to hunt.

FATHER

(smiling)

Oh! Let me show you another great hunter.

He takes her to a picture on the wall.

FATHER (cont'd)

Do you know who this is?

The picture shows Nicholas, at a young age, sitting on an elephant's back, crying.

ELAINA

Oh.

(goes next to Nicholas)

How cute!

FATHER

(in a serious tone)

Nicholas never liked hunting. He loves the water, boating, fishing, and sailing.

Nicholas jumps on the opportunity to join the conversation.

NICHOLAS

Yes, I do. As a matter of fact, Elaina and I would like to go to our Geneva house and stay, maybe for good.

Of course, if it is okay with you both.

FATHER

And what are your plans, son?

NICHOLAS

Well, first we plan to get married.

(they are holding hands)

I can set up my practice there.

FATHER

(interrupting)

You always liked that small, quiet town, didn't you?

NICHOLAS

(continuing)

We want to have a family and stay there year-round. Make it our home if it's okay.

FATHER

(looking at his wife)

Son, I know you love that place.

(he puffs his pipe, walking a few steps back and forth)

Nobody goes there anyway. Your mother and I have
not been there for months.

(MORE)

FATHER

(he looks at his wife, listening and nodding her head as if to say to
him, I agree)

Do I hear you saying you plan to get married and
have a family? Soon, I hope.

NICHOLAS

Yes, sir, very soon!

FATHER

And have children!

NICHOLAS

Yes, sir.

FATHER

(looks at both of them and puffs his pipe)

I have a feeling you will make a good couple. It's all
yours.

Nicholas and Elaina both jump with happiness. They never expected
it to be so easy.

NICHOLAS & ELAINA

(together)

Thank you, Dad. Thank you, Mom.

The four of them hug and kiss.

FATHER

(trying to cover his emotional feelings)

Now, you two go ahead. I have work to do.

(walks back to his step ladder)

They thank him again, and the three of them turn around toward
the door.

FATHER

Listen!

(they all stop)

It will be nice for myself and mother to have some little ones to come visit and play with from time to time! And frankly, I am getting bored being around them all the time.

(points to the animals)

NICHOLAS

(smiling)

I promise you that, and so does Elaina.

ELAINA

(in a low voice)

Yes, yes, I promise too.

They both hug and kiss Mother as she hands them the keys to their new house, and they run out to the car, holding hands. Mother follows them outside.

MOTHER

Be careful.

(waves goodbye and throws kisses)

NICHOLAS

You can come and visit us. Okay, Mom?

ELAINA

Often, please.

They drive away.

The sun is about to hide behind the trees on the other side of the lake when they pull into the narrow driveway of their new home.

Nicholas gets out, followed by Elaina, opens the door, and gets the luggage out of the car. He goes up a few steps, opens the front door of the house, and turns on the lights.

ELAINA

(looking around)

It's beautiful.

NICHOLAS

(happy, with satisfaction)

Isn't it? Come and see all of it.

He walks toward the balcony door. He pulls the drapes open and unlocks the door. A breathtaking view of a beautiful lake is in front of them and a gentle breeze rushes into the house, blowing the drapes back and forth.

Nicholas takes a deep breath as he steps outside on the balcony. They stand there for a while, Elaina holds Nicholas's arm with both of her hands.

ELAINA

(in a low voice, looking at the sun going down)

It's so beautiful! So Beautiful!

They walk back into the house, still holding hands.

NICHOLAS

(shows her the rooms)

Our kitchen has a view of the lake.

ELAINA

(standing in front of the sink)

Oh. Yes. What a view!

NICHOLAS

This is the study room. Here is where I am going to set up my drawing board.

(MORE)

NICHOLAS

I'll be working with my drawings, looking once outside at the lake and once at you, my love!

(they hug and kiss for some time)

In the bedroom, Elaina is still asleep, while Nicholas is awake. He looks at Elaina sleeping. She is beautiful. He smiles and silently gets up, puts his slippers on, and walks to the kitchen.

He opens a cabinet and finds a box of tea. He throws a bag in a pot and fills it with water. He turns the stove on and lets it boil.

Then he fills a cup with tea and walks outside to the balcony. He sits on the hanging wicker love seat and, sipping the hot tea, enjoys the lake view.

Elaina wakes up and sees that Nicholas is already out of bed. She whispers his name and gets up herself.

The door to the balcony is open, and the drapes are dancing as a soft breeze is coming through the door.

Elaina smells the aroma of the tea. She rushes to the balcony. Elaina sits on Nicholas's lap and kisses him good morning.

ELAINA

Did you sleep well?

NICHOLAS

Oh, yes!

ELAINA

Did you have any dreams? Do you dream?

NICHOLAS

Of course, I have dreams. I had a dream that I was
sleeping next to a beautiful girl!

Elaina smiles. She gives him another kiss.

ELAINA

Thank you.

    (they sit for a while, then a boat passes by.)

Look, Nicholas. That is a nice boat.

NICHOLAS

It's a thirty-two or thirty-four- footer, a beautiful
boat.

Then an even bigger boat goes by. She is excited to watch the boats.

ELAINA

Here is another one. It is so beautiful, so lovely, and so
peaceful and romantic here.

    (she gets up)

NICHOLAS

The name of the boat is *The Lady of the Lake* tour
boat.

(he gets up, lays his hands on her back)

Let's get ready. We will go down, and you will get a chance to see them closer.

Nicholas walks to the door, pulling Elaina gently. She is fascinated by looking at the *Lady of the Lake*. She follows him slowly inside.

Wearing shorts, they walk out holding hands. They stop at the observation deck, at ground level.

NICHOLAS

(points to the lake below as more and more boats appear—motor and sail boats.)

Look!

(MORE)

NICHOLAS

From this point, you can see the whole lake. To the left is the village of Fontana, and to the right is the town.

ELAINA

What a breathtaking view. What a nice breeze.

NICHOLAS

This, my dear, is the breeze of love. Our love.

They stand there for a while, feeling the soft breeze and holding hands and kissing.

NICHOLAS

Let's go down by the piers to see where all the boats are docked.

ELAINA

Let's go!

They run down the steps, holding hands.

They walk to the first pier, where on both sides of them, boats are being lifted up on their hoists.

At the end of the pier, Elaina waves to the passengers of the boats going by, and they wave back to her. Some blow their horns. She loves it.

From that day on, they go down to the piers daily, watching the magnificent sunsets and the boats going by.

They sit down at the end of the pier with their feet splashing the water, playing, counting the baby fish in the water, and feeling the breeze, the lovely breeze.

Having fun, Nicholas jumps into the water, shows off his swimming abilities, and Elaina admires him.

Elaina learns to fish from the pier, and Nicholas shows her how to hook her bait.

NICHOLAS

Here.

(MORE)

NICHOLAS

(he takes a worm and puts it through the hook)

Simple!

ELAINA

No, I can't do this.

(she looks in the other direction)

Nicholas shows her how to release the line and explains that when she feels a bite, she rolls her line up.

NICHOLAS

Okay?

ELAINA

Okay.

NICHOLAS

Over here. This looks like a nice spot.

(he drops the line in and hands it to Elaina)

And now you stay here and wait for a bite.
Remember, when you feel the bite, roll it up nice and
easy. Okay?

ELAINA

(moves her head up and down)

Yes.

Elaina holds the rod with both hands, anxiously looking at the water,
and she raises the rod when she feels a bite.

Nicholas is further down at the end of the pier.

He throws his line far, like an expert fisherman.

Suddenly, Elaina calls with all the power in her lungs and shouts.

ELAINA

Nicholas. Nicholas. I got one. I got a big one. I got it.

Nicholas puts his rod down and runs toward her. Elaina is so excited,
like a kid.

ELAINA

My first fish. I got it.

Nicholas helps her. He pulls out the end of the line. There, a very,
very small fish is hanging.

FALL COMES, THE LEAVES ARE CHANGING COLORS.
THE SUNSETS ARE BEAUTIFUL. THEY TAKE LONG
WALKS ON THE SHORE OF THE WATER.

Nicholas works on his designs. Elaina brings him tea and hugs and kisses him.

They laugh, they play, and she sings to him as she washes dishes. They are so happy together.

INT. – AT HOME – EVENING

They have their first Christmas together.

They are both decorating and hanging all kinds of ornaments. She does most of the work.

ELAINA

Here, Nicholas, here. Please bring the step ladder over for me.

Nicholas brings the ladder.

ELAINA

Closer here.

(MORE)

ELAINA

(points to a spot above the fireplace)

The Christmas wreath will look beautiful here. Don't you think so?

Nicholas looks up and agrees. He makes a funny face. Elaina places the step ladder against the wall. She backs up.

ELAINA

Hold it up there, between the ceiling and the ledge of the fireplace. Go ahead. Go on, Nicholas. I want to see how it looks.

Nicholas hesitates for a moment. He slowly walks to the ladder. He goes up the first step, then the second, he looks up, then the third. He holds himself with both hands. Up another step.

Elaina, laughing hysterically, goes by the ladder and shakes it a little.

ELAINA

You're afraid. You are afraid of heights, aren't you?

NICHOLAS

(scared)

Yes.

(he comes down from the ladder)

ELAINA

(Elaina laughs and hugs him)

You never told me that.

The wreath is up, the fire is in the fireplace, the Christmas tree is beautifully decorated, and the Christmas lights are on.

They have company. The four guests are Nicholas's parents, George, and Big Daddy.

After dinner is served, Nicholas breaks the big news.

NICHOLAS

Elaina is expecting a baby!

The news is received with great joy, cheers, champagne, and kisses.

During the rest of the winter months, Elaina and Nicholas go skating and snowmobiling on the frozen lake.

As a passenger, Elaina finds snowmobiling to be a great, exciting experience. Nicholas always drives carefully, keeping in mind that his wife is expecting.

One day, on one of their excursions, Elaina, overwhelmed with excitement, demonstrates her acrobatic skills. She stands up behind Nicholas, who is driving rather fast. She extends her arms to the sides.

Leaning forward over him she has her hands free and extended at her sides.

ELAINA

(yells with enthusiasm)

I am a bird! A flying bird! An ice bird!

(she laughs as Nicholas, fearful, slows down and reminds her)

NICHOLAS

Please don't. Don't do that. Remember the baby.

EXT. - SUMMER - PIER

The boats are in the clear lake water. There are all kinds of boats. Elaina admires all of them, but especially the sailboats with their full-blown sails.

ELAINA

What a sight, and what a lovely breeze.

(MORE)

ELAINA

(she whispers, standing by her husband)

NICHOLAS

(placing his arms around her, he replies with a smile in a low voice)

It's the breeze of love, my love. The breeze of our
love!

Elaina turns to face Nicholas, and with a smile full of love, she hugs
and kisses him, patting his hair with one of her hands.

ELAINA

How nicely put together, Nicholas! It is the breeze of
our love, darling.

(they kiss again)

One day, early in the morning, while Elaina is still sleeping, Nicholas
gets up, dresses, and quietly leaves the house. When Elaina wakes
up, she calls for Nicholas, and after getting no response, she becomes
worried.

She is nervous, and she walks out on the balcony, looks around, and
calls for him again. She walks in and out of the house to the balcony,
wondering if there is a note for her.

Time goes by. Two whole hours and no sight of Nicholas. She calls
his mom, but there is no answer. Finally, down from the piers,
Nicholas's voice is heard calling her name. She runs to the balcony.

ELAINA

(with a loud voice)

Nicholas, where are you? Are you all right?

FAR AWAY VOICE

(he calls to her)

Come down. Come on down!

Elaina runs out and down the steps to the piers.

FAR AWAY VOICE

Over here. Here on the third pier.

She runs as directed to the dock. Nicholas is standing up on a white sailboat, wearing a white captain's hat. His arms are extended at his sides when Elaina shows up.

NICHOLAS

Tada! I present to you, my honey, your boat!

ELAINA

(relieved that he is okay) (she is out of breath)

Nicholas.

(she says once she has a feeling of relief that Nicholas is all right and once she has a feeling of happiness, realizing what Nicholas has done)

Nicholas.

On the side of the boat, the name *Breeze of Love* is written.

Elaina places her hands on her face. She's standing by the edge of the pier. She cries from happiness.

NICHOLAS

Come on board, my dear. Come, jump in.

Elaina hesitates at the beginning, but with Nicholas's help, she jumps on the *Breeze of Love*.

Nicholas raises the sails, and they go for their first ride.

ELAINA

(from time to time)

Oh, my God! I don't believe it.

(turns to him)

Our own boat? I can't believe it.

(MORE)

ELAINA

(as she hugs and kisses him, she shouts)

I love you! I love you!

She is like a little kid with her first toy. She waves to boaters passing by.

ELAINA

(loud)

This is our boat—our own boat!

The *Breeze of Love* brings more happiness to this couple, who are in love.

ELAINA

You know, we don't have to watch other boats
anymore and dream and fantasize; we have our own!

Their dreams came true. They sailed when the sun was rising, in the middle of hot days, and at sunset.

The most romantic times of their lives were sailing on the *Breeze of Love*.

She sits next to him or lies in his lap, enjoying the smooth sailing, whispering a tune, or sometimes really singing a song.

IT WAS A BEAUTIFUL MIDDAY IN AUGUST.

Nicholas finishes his work early, and the young couple walk down to the piers.

Elaina is only two weeks away from having the baby. Carefully, she puts her life preserver on, and with Nicholas's help, she gets on the boat.

She sits down next to the steering wheel. Nicholas unties the boat and raises up the sails. The lake breeze is blowing gently, and they start on an enjoyable, smooth, romantic ride.

Some sailboats that are passing by are blowing their horns and some people on others are waving.

A small boat with younger people on board, driving rather fast, going left and right, cut in front of the *Breeze of Love*. This is not a good thing since boaters know that a motor boat shouldn't cut in front of a sailboat at close range.

The youngsters are laughing and making all kinds of gestures, knowing what they have done is bad game. They drive away fast. Nicholas gets up from his seat and shakes his head.

NICHOLAS

(as he was about to sit back down next to Elaina, he whispers)

Those damn kids! Weekend boaters!

Elaina looks at him, smiles, and gives him a kiss on the cheek.

ELAINA

(looking at Nicholas with happiness and satisfaction)

Captain Nicholas! Papa to be!

He looks at her with a smile full of love, and they keep sailing, holding hands. Elaina leans toward him, touching his face with her cheek.

ELAINA

I love you with all my heart.

NICHOLAS

I love you now and forever.

They keep sailing north, not paying any attention to the small boat with the youngsters they had encountered before, who are riding at high speed, going in any and every direction.

They did not realize that those youngsters, crossing behind a big cruiser at a very high speed, have been thrown off the boat into the water, and now their boat, with no driver, is going dangerously fast and heading in their direction.

Before they knew what was hitting them, there is a tremendous collision. The unmanned boat crashes into the side of *The Breeze of Love*, breaks it into pieces, and throws both Nicholas and Elaina into the lake. An explosion of the motor boat follows, and there are gas and flames all around them.

After a while, Elaina appears, fighting the waves and the hell around her, trying to get away, fighting for her life, and yelling for Nicholas.

ELAINA

Nicholas! Nicholas! Nicholas! Where are you? Are you all right? Nicholas...

(yelling over and over, again and again and again)

There is no sign of Nicholas anywhere. Only his torn life preserver appears to be floating in the water. Nicholas is nowhere to be found. He had vanished into the deep water.

Boats and the rescue squad are around the side. They rescue Elaina. She is unconscious. They pick up Nicholas's life jacket. The straps are broken.

Ah, this is irony. This is the end of a very strong love between two lovely people and the end of a life full of dreams—a dream of love that is cut short with a sudden ending in the deep waters of the lake they loved so much.

INT. HOSPITAL - AFTERNOON

In the hospital's waiting room, Nicholas's parents, Big Daddy, and George are anxiously waiting for news on Elaina's condition.

Finally, a doctor, escorted by two nurses, appears to be coming out of the operating room located at the end of the hallway.

They all jump up as they see the three of them approaching.

DOCTOR

Mom and son are doing well. It will be a little while before you can see them.

(they walk away)

Elaina is lying with her eyes closed when Nicholas' parents, Big Daddy, and George are allowed to enter her hospital room.

When Nicholas's mother pats her hand, she slowly opens her eyes and starts crying, looking at each one of them.

ELAINA

(in agony)

Why, why, why?

BIG DADDY

Everything will be okay, honey. Everything will be okay.

ELAINA

My baby. My baby. May I see my baby?

(to the nurse in the room who was standing by her)

The nurse leaves the room and returns shortly with a beautiful new bornbaby. She places the baby in Elaina's arms.

ELAINA

Nicholas. Oh, Nicholas. Where are you?

(kisses the baby's head)

Here is your son, Nicholas. Where are you?

The nurse approaches, takes the baby out of Elaina's hands, pats her on the head, and asks her to please rest now.

She turns to the rest of the people and kindly asks them to leave and let Elaina rest.

EXT. HOME - AFTERNOON

On the balcony, sitting on the swing, Elaina is holding in baby Nicholas in her arms, looking at the lake and reminiscing.

Nicholas's mother is cooking in the kitchen. His father comes in from the balcony and tries to cheer her up.

FATHER

There is a delicious cake inside for you. Mother baked it. A family recipe.

LITTLE NICHOLAS IS GROWING, HE IS ALMOST THREE AND ONE-HALF YEARS OLD.

George makes frequent visits, plays with the toddler, teaches him balloon tricks, and how to make animals with them.

Big Daddy brings Little Nicholas all kinds of presents, despite Elaina's complaints that he spoils him.

Elaina and Little Nicholas live alone in the lake house with the support of Nicholas's parents and a part-time job as an assistant in gymnastics at the park district.

Elaina keeps Little Nicholas at the gym by her side and helps him work on the parallel bars.

At night, she puts Little Nicholas to bed, reads him stories, and helps him with his prayers, asking God to look after his dad, who is up in heaven. She kisses him good night, tells him how much she loves him. She lies on her bed across from Little Nicholas's room, going through a book full of pictures of her and her husband, or herself as a little girl, and of her life in the circus.

ELAINA

Guess who is coming to visit us today?

Big Daddy's visits were a big, exciting time, not only for Little Nicholas but for Elaina too.

LITTLE NICHOLAS

My Big Daddy.

ELAINA

No! No! My big daddy, your big grandpa.

(Making a face at him)

They are both excited in anticipation of his visit and when they hear the car pulling into the driveway, they jump with happiness.

ELAINA AND LITTLE NICHOLAS

(yelling)

He's here! He's here!

They run to the door and welcome him with a big hug and kisses.

Big Daddy takes Little Nicholas in his arms and carries him in the house, listening to the child's achievements since the previous visit.

Uncle George will surprise them with his frequent visits, announcing his arrivals by blowing his funny sounding musical horn. He entertains Nicholas with his magic tricks, helps Elaina around the house, takes them out to the ice cream parlor, and from time to time presents Elaina with a bouquet of roses that he hides inside his jacket and whispers to her.

GEORGE

With all my love.

Elaina innocently kisses him on the cheek.

During visits from Big Daddy, Elaina asks questions about life and the people at the circus.

ELAINA

How are things at the circus? How is Pierre doing? Is he mad at me?

BIG DADDY

He misses you very much.

Pierre has never been able to find another partner as good as you, for as much as he has tried.

You were a natural.

The two of you were the best.

ELAINA

Thank you. Say hello to everybody from me.
Someday I will come and visit.

BIG DADDY

(nodding his head up and down)

Please do.

At night, after putting Little Nicholas to bed, she sits in the reclining
chair where her husband used to sit and lets her mind go back to the
circus.

She thinks of the Grand March with all the performers and
herself standing on the back of an elephant, waving to the crowd
that's applauding with excitement, and Nicholas standing up and
applauding with enthusiasm.

She hears the band playing, the impressive Big Daddy announcing
the acts, Pierre and herself performing their amazing acrobatic acts,
etc.

She talks to Little Nicholas about all these things. She shows him
pictures of the place where she grew up and of the performances of
her circus family.

ELAINA

You know your mother was a great acrobat before you
were born.

People used to love and applaud her every time she performed.

Someday we are going to visit Grand Daddy, and I will show you around where I grew up.

(MORE)

ELAINA

We might stay there for a while.

There are ponies, elephants, and children to play with.

EXT. HOME/YARD – MORNING

One morning, Elaina packs her station wagon with some of her and her child's personal belongings and drives to the circus.

As she pulls into the circus driveway, several of the circus people recognize her and come toward her car.

Elaina rolls her windows down, stops her car, and they start shaking hands, talking, and kissing hello to each other.

She parks the car and gets out. She helps Little Nicholas out of his car seat.

A couple of ladies tries to pick up Little Nicholas. He refuses to be picked up and huddles closer to his mother. He is startled and frightened a little.

CIRCUS LADIES

(happy and shouting)

Elaina is back.

FIRST CIRCUS LADY

(runs to Pierre's door and knocks, calling)

Elaina is here. She's back!

As Elaina, with the crowd, walks up the trailer path, Pierre's door opens, showing him standing in the opening with no expression on his face.

ELAINA

(stops and looks at Pierre)

Hello, Pierre.

PIERRE

Are you back?

ELAINA

(nods her head with a smile)

Yes, Pierre. I'm back.

Pierre's attitude changes; he comes down the two steps of the trailer smiling, comes to Elaina, bows in front of her, and holds his hands up.

PIERRE

Welcome back to the family.

They both hug each other in a friendly way. Little Nicholas looks up at his Mom, and the people around him are applauding.

INT. CIRCUS TENT - EVENING

As the applause continues, we are transferred to the circus tent, showing the circus audience applauding for Elaina and Pierre, who are being announced by Big Daddy.

Their act starts. From then on, the circus is in big glory again, with Elaina and Pierre performing their breathtaking acrobatic acts.

Every time Elaina is going to start her act, she peeks between the curtains where they meet at the center of the stage, looking at the spot where Nicholas used to sit.

ELAINA

(whispers)

I love you.

(goes on with her act)

In his spare time, Big Grandpa takes Little Nicholas for a pony ride or to play with the monkeys, little lambs, or other circus animals.

Before Elaina performs, she puts Little Nicholas down for a nap in the trailer and reassures him she will be back very soon.

Little Nicholas pretends he is falling asleep, and soon after Elaina leaves, he gets up and takes the picture of his mother with his father, hugs it, kisses it, and says a prayer to God.

PIERRE

(still desiring a more dangerous act that will make him famous)

You know, our act is getting boring. It's kind of monotonous—the same act over and over.

We have mastered the double flip all right. Let's try something more exciting. Let's try the triple flip.

ELAINA

Oh no. It is much too dangerous. Thank you, but it's almost impossible.

You know, Violet? The last performer who tried that in Europe fell to her death!

So did Martha before her.

PIERRE

(interrupts her)

But no one was like you and me. No one. These
hands are like a vice. They can stop a falling elephant,
and you are as light as a feather.

Let's give it a try just for the fun of it.

They both climb up and swing a few times.

(VIEWED IN SLOW MOTION) ELAINA JUMPS, FOLLOWED
BY ONE, TWO, AND THE IMPOSSIBLE THIRD FLIP AND
MISSES PIERRE'S HANDS.

She falls onto the safety net under her. This makes Pierre upset.

PIERRE

(insisting)

Let's try again, now!

ELAINA

Oh, no. Please.

PIERRE

Damn it. Back up. For sure, we almost had it. Climb
this time. We can do it.

Elaina climbs up and tries again, but falls onto the safety net. After
that, determined to stop practicing, she jumps down from the net
and walks away.

They tried a couple of other times, against Elaina's wishes, but they did not succeed.

Every time they practiced, Pierre insisted on trying again, sometimes succeeding and sometimes not.

Big Daddy observed them and did not approve of it. He confronted Pierre.

                    BIG DADDY

What are you trying to do?

It's the most dangerous act.

Nobody has mastered it, and you know what
happened to people who tried it, Pierre.

I don't approve of it. It's impossible.

                    PIERRE

It's not impossible. Who says it's impossible? We have
mastered it.

We have been doing it without failure lately.

                    BIG DADDY

I don't care.

                    (MORE)

BIG DADDY (cont'd)

I don't approve of it. It's too risky and dangerous
without a net.

A failure can destroy us all. I am not about to
jeopardize Elaina's life for all the gold or fame in the
world.

I don't approve it.

(he starts walking away from Pierre)

PIERRE

Okay, okay. I'll settle with you. I'll do it with a net.

(he whispers sarcastically)

Well, we will do it.

INT. CIRCUS - EVENING

The show had already started under the great tent of the circus.
Suddenly, the weather outside is rapidly changing, and a dangerous
storm is developing.

Elaina and Pierre are up on the platform, ready to perform.

The wind is getting stronger and stronger. The walls of the tent are
moving dangerously. The lights are flickering on and off, and the
whole tent is shaking. People, scared, started to leave quietly.

Big Daddy, on the microphone, tries to calm them down.

BIG DADDY

Folks, don't worry. Just a storm going over. We are
safe here.

NOW PEOPLE IN PANIC START RUNNING OUT
THROUGH THE EXITS.

As Elaina and Pierre start sliding down the ropes, the storm is getting
stronger.

The whole tent is moving dangerously.

The center pole sways left and right, breaking off the supporting
ropes.

The performers are gathering up their belongings as the canvas of the
tent is tearing apart. The force of the wind picks up items that are
loose on the stage.

Outside, a couple of the smaller trailers are tipped over.

Elaina, scared for her child, runs out toward her trailer. She is
fighting the force of the storm and keeping going.

By the time she gets close to her trailer, the trailer door is open,
slamming in the wind.

Elaina rushes in.

ELAINA

Nicholas! Nicholas, where are you?

She looks around all the rooms and under the beds

ELAINA

Oh, my baby, my baby!

Little Nicholas, worried about his mother, had run out looking
for her, and he left the door open, and the wind caught it. He was
thrown around by the force of the wind, all over, while crying for
his mom.

Items and boxes are rolling loose, blown all over between the trailers
and the tent.

The main pole, with all of its supporting ropes broken, falls across
the trailer road, dragging big pieces of canvas with it and covering
Little Nicholas under it.

Elaina, not finding Little Nicholas in the trailer, desperately runs out.

ELAINA

(screaming with despair, she runs down the road, calling)

Nicholas, Nicholas, Nicholas!

Finally, she hears Nicholas crying, calling for her, coming out of
someplace where the big pole landed.

LITTLE NICHOLAS

(tearfully)

Mommy, Mommy, Mommy.

Elaina storms to the direction where his voice is coming from,
calling his name.

ELAINA

(as loud as she can scream)

Nicholas, Nicholas, Nicholas!

She pushes aside pieces of canvas and wood and lifts more canvas.

She crawls under and finds him lying under the pole that
mysteriously had stopped before crushing him to death.

Elaina, with Little Nicholas in her arms, muddy and bleeding, crawls
out and runs toward her trailer.

Little Nicholas, looking back to where he was found, keeps trying
and repeating.

LITTLE NICHOLAS

Mommy, Mommy, Daddy, Daddy, Mommy, My
Daddy...

INT. TRAILER - EVENING

Finally, they get to the trailer and she secures the door behind them.

She sits him on a chair and, with a towel, tries to dry him up. She kisses him and checks him for cuts or bruises.

ELAINA

(asking him constantly)

Are you all right, son? Are you okay, my baby?

After the storms pass through and Little Nicholas calms down, laying in his mother's lap, he is pointing toward the outside, trying to say something, mentioning the word.

LITTLE NICHOLAS

Daddy, My Daddy.

(he keeps on repeating)

ELAINA

(stops and looks at him)

Nicholas. Are you talking about Daddy?

LITTLE NICHOLAS

(pointing outside)

Over there! out there! My Daddy.

ELAINA

Where Nicholas? Was Daddy out there?

LITTLE NICHOLAS

Yes.

(Shakes his head up and down to say yes.)

ELAINA

With you?

LITTLE NICHOLAS

Mmm, hmm. My daddy.

She picks him up, crying and repeating.

ELAINA

Daddy was with you? Oh, my, God! Oh, my, God!

She sits on the bed, holding him in her arms, silently. Tears are rolling down her cheeks from her eyes. She kisses Little Nicholas on the head, patting him and repeating.

ELAINA

Oh, Nicholas. I know you are with us. I love you now
and forever.

EXT. CIRCUS VILLAGE - MORNING

The sun is shining again.

Big Daddy goes out of his trailer and walks down the path, sizing up with his eyes the horrible results of the previous night's storm.

As if the people of the circus have been waiting for him to pass by their trailers, they open their doors immediately and follow him.

This stream of humans follows him, as if he were their only hope. Among them is Elaina, holding Little Nicholas in her arms.

Big Daddy stops by the spot where the big pole that was broken is lying.

He gets up on a wooden box. The followers stop too, staring and waiting to see what he has to say.

                    BIG DADDY

    Okay, everybody. We have a lot of work to do here.
    We are going to overcome this terrible catastrophe.

            (he looks up at the sky)

    It's a beautiful day today.

            (in a lower voice)

    It is always nice after the storm.

    We have learned to laugh and cry together. That is
    the life of the circus people.

Together, we are going to work hard and rebuild this place, as always, as one family. We shall overcome this catastrophe. Let's get to work.

THE CROWD

Yes, let's get to work now!

After that, they all started picking up and cleaning up the refuse.

As a result of the terrible ordeal that Little Nicholas has experienced, he develops a phobia.

He wants to be with his mom at all times.

LITTLE NICHOLAS

(crying as she gets ready for her performance)

Please, Mommy, don't go. Don't do your act anymore.

ELAINA

(trying to comfort him)

Don't worry sweetie.

Mother loves you a lot.

Nothing can happen to me.

There is a net under me when I jump.

Your daddy is watching us from heaven, and he protects me.

LITTLE NICHOLAS

I don't want you to jump anymore. Please, Mom, don't! I'm scared for you.

ELAINA

I know. That's the same thing your father used to say.

Pierre is insisting on performing the dangerous triple flip that will make them famous. Nothing that Elaina says makes him change his mind.

BIG DADDY

Are you going to go with that crazy, impossible triple flip?

PIERRE

Yes, yes, we are going to do it.

The triple flip will be performed at the re-opening night after we finish rebuilding the grounds.

As a matter of fact, you can advertise that.

Put that in the papers, on television, everywhere for the reopening night.

Great suggestion, eh?

BIG DADDY

(shakes his head "no" as he walks away)

Only with the safety net. Let that be clear. Only with the net.

EXT. CIRCUS GROUNDS - EVENING

The re-opening night is here. Everything is ready.

The announcement of the new act brings a big crowd, including photographers, reporters, and dignitaries.

Big Daddy is dressed in his impressive red outfit with his ringmaster's hat.

There are the lights, the music, the ropes, and big posters featuring the different acts, and every participant is ready.

The doors to the big tent are open, and George, as usual, is there directing people to their seats, making animal shapes and hats with balloons for the youngsters, and kidding around with the audience.

The show starts on time.

Behind the curtain, performers are pacing back and forth.

Pierre, who is kind of nervous, is stretching to loosen up.

CIRCUS WORKER #1

(to Pierre)

Where is Elaina?

PIERRE

(sarcastically)

I don't know. Probably with her kid.

Elaina is still in her trailer, dressed for the performance, holding Little Nicholas up in her arms and lecturing to him.

ELAINA

Look, you know Mother loves you. Don't you?

LITTLE NICHOLAS

Yes.

(nods his head, paying more attention to the cross on his mother's neck)

ELAINA

Play with your toys until I come back. Work your puzzle we bought.

(she puts him down)

Let's start it together.

(sits on the floor and puts some pieces together, trying to motivate him)

Little Nicholas goes along, placing some pieces together.

Elaina looks at the clock.

ELAINA

Mommy has to go now. I will be back soon. Very soon. Be a good boy now, and remember that Mother loves you very, very much.

(MORE)

ELAINA

(she kisses him and gets up)

Nicholas stays on the floor with his head down.

ELAINA

I am coming back soon. I promise.

Nicholas's head goes farther down, and tears are rolling down his face.

ELAINA

(sits down again)

Oh, baby, don't cry! This is a very important day for me!

LITTLE NICHOLAS

(whispering)

Please, Mom, don't go! Please Mom!

ELAINA

I have to. I'll be back soon. I promise.

She makes the sign of the cross, kneels in front of her icon by the dresser, and prays, as she always does before performing.

ELAINA

I will be back...I will be back. I love you. I promise you.

(leaves the trailer with a broken heart)

Little Nicholas is alone in the trailer. He gets up, takes the picture of his mom and dad from the dresser, climbs up in his bed, places the picture next to him, and lies down with tears still rolling down his cheeks.

INT. CIRCUS TENT - EVENING

Elaina rushes behind the stage.

Pierre looks at her coldly.

Elaina looks disturbed. She stretches a few times and shakes her arms and head a few times to loosen up.

CIRCUS DIRECTOR

(passing by)

You are next. Good luck.

Elaina and Pierre keep stretching.

Elaina then walks to the curtain and peeks out where her husband used to sit.

Pierre looks at her and continues his warm-up routine.

BIG DADDY

(In center of stage, announces)

And now, ladies and gentlemen, tonight's finale of the great Elaina and Pierre in their death-defying act.

Pierre walks up behind Elaina.

PIERRE

(talking fast)

Let's go. It's time for us.

They walk out. People are applauding.

They bow and start climbing up the ropes while Big Daddy announces.

BIG DADDY

(in a lower voice than usual)

Ladies and gentlemen, what you are about to witness is a historical event.

It's the most critical and the most dangerous act ever performed.

For the first time in two decades, it will be attempted here at the Tripolink Circus.

(MORE)

BIG DADDY

It is the impossible triple flip.

Ladies and gentlemen, please keep absolute silence.
Please wish them good luck!

As Big Daddy finishes the announcement about the historical triple flip and walks away from the stage, two of the circus assistants (instructed by Pierre) run out and remove the safety net, to Big Daddy's surprise.

But it is too late for Big Daddy to do anything.

BIG DADDY

(Furious pacing back stage)

Traitor! Son of a bitch!

The couple is about to reach the landing platform. Elaina is climbing slower than normally. She keeps Little Nicholas's image in her mind as he tells her not to go. She also sees her husband's image. She hears in her mind.

LITTLE NICHOLAS

Please Mom, don't go...Please Mom...We need you, please.

These thoughts are haunting her all the way to the platform, and she starts swinging on the bars.

She is fighting with both images.

ELAINA

(talking to herself)

I know, I know...But for the last time, maybe, I have to do it.

And again, her husband's image is very vivid. She even hears him speaking.

NICHOLAS

For the love of our child, don't jump, please.

She sees Little Nicholas's image crying under the broken tent the night of the storm.

The act starts. They salute the audience.

Pierre jumps on the bar first. He swings back and forth, hanging down from the bar, supported by his knees.

Elaina follows by making the same moves as Pierre, but she is still showing signs of not being all put together. She skips one of the exchanges (from their routine warm- up act) as she jumps.

PIERRE

(upset)

Get with it! Get with it! Be with me. Time it.

They went on with their normal exchanges and acts.

The drums of the band are getting louder and more dramatic as the time gets closer for the biggest act on earth.

Elaina swing back and forth on the horizontal bar, sees the image of the two Nicholas in her mind. She looks down on the stage..

Performers and every member of the circus gather behind Big Daddy, looking with apprehension and fear.

Big Daddy is making the sign of the cross.

George is very intense and is anxiously walking up the aisle.

There is absolute silence in the audience as Elaina swings back and forth in a slower rhythm.

Pierre looks at her, worried. He claps his hands. He is ready for the big moment.

PIERRE

Come on. Get with it! Your timing. Your rhythm.

(next time they cross)

Come on, let's do it now.

Elaina, ignoring the command, keeps on swinging mechanically, and instead of pursuing the dangerous triple flip, jumps up on the platform.

Elaina stands there for a few moments, and while everybody's eyes are fixed on her, she starts sliding down the rope, leaving a stunned Pierre on his bar, swinging.

The circus audience is disappointed, and they are booing her.

As she reaches the ground, she runs backstage, picks up her robe from where it was hanging on the wall, exits, and keeps running, pushing everyone out of her way.

CIRCUS AUDIENCE

(as they are leaving, some are saying)

She chickened out. What a disappointment. She got scared.

Elaina continues running until she reaches her trailer. She opens the door and rushes in.

Little Nicholas has fallen asleep with the picture of his mom and dad lying next to him on his pillow.

Elaina lays in his bed next to him, kisses him a few times, and breaks into a cry.

Pierre, furious, is knocking at her door. Getting no answer, he proceeds to leave.

PIERRE

You are a coward.

I know you can hear me.

You are a big coward. Coward!

What an embarrassment.

Pierre leaves, walking down to the tent. He is stopped by a group of circus people.

PIERRE

(explaining)

I don't know what the hell happened to her. She was never scared before.

(walks away holding his head)

I cannot get over the embarrassment.

INT. ELAINA'S TRAILER - NEXT MORNING

Elaina is awake and preparing a meal for Little Nicholas.

Some voices from outside (the voices of kids) are heard.

KIDS' VOICES

Elaina is a coward! She is a coward.

Elaina stops for a minute and looks at Little Nicholas, who sleeping. Some of the kids are coming over, standing close by her door, sticking their faces on the window, and yelling.

KIDS' VOICES

Coward! Coward! Elaina is a coward!

Little Nicholas begins to wake up. Elaina goes to him.

ELAINA

Hello! My goodness. You slept for eleven hours.

Little Nicholas looks around, looks at his mom, and cracks a smile. As she picks him up, he rubs his face on her and stays still for a while.

ELAINA

Come. Let's sit at the table.

(she takes him and puts him down on a chair)

Would you like cinnamon toast with peanut butter and jelly or cereal with strawberries?

LITTLE NICHOLAS

(nods his head up and down)

Yes.

ELAINA

Cereal with strawberries.

LITTLE NICHOLAS

Okay.

Elaina serves the bowl.

Little Nicholas takes a spoon and starts eating.

Elaina sits on a chair by the table and watches him in silence.

Little Nicholas finishes eating.

ELAINA

I am going to jump in the shower.

When I am through, we will play together, okay?

In the meantime, take this coloring book and your crayons and color a nice picture for me.

Elaina proceeds to the shower, and shortly after she comes out, wrapped in her robe.

Not yet over the drama of last night, she plays cards with Little Nicholas, and later on they are putting together a puzzle.

As time goes by, the doorbell rings, and Big Daddy's face appears in the little window in the door. They both jump as she opens the door, and Little Nicholas runs over to him. Big Daddy is dressed up in his stage outfit.

The boy is excited to see him. He jumps on Big Daddy's lap.

LITTLE NICHOLAS

Grandpa, Grandpa!

(kisses him)

BIG DADDY

How is my boy?

Little Nicholas points to the puzzle he is working on.

BIG DADDY

You did all these?

Oh, my goodness. You are a smart boy, aren't you?

LITTLE NICHOLAS

(agrees)

Mmm, hmmm. Mmm, hmmm.

Big Daddy looks at Elaina.

BIG DADDY

And how are you, young lady?

Elaina pauses and shows her sad feelings.

ELAINA

Okay, considering...

LITTLE NICHOLAS

(to Big Daddy)

Are you going to take me out for a pony ride, Grandpa?

BIG DADDY

Not now.

(looking at Elaina)

The matinee starts in half an hour.

Sorry, I have no time today. As a matter of fact, I have to go very soon.

He kisses the boy, waves goodbye to Elaina, and leaves the trailer.

INT. CIRCUS TENT

Soon, the music from the circus is heard playing, and then Big Daddy's voice welcoming the audience is heard on the loud speaker.

Elaina looks at the clock. She is nervous. She stops playing with Little Nicholas.

Slowly, she gets up, goes by the window, and looks toward the direction of the big tent.

Gently, she picks up Little Nicholas and sits him by the edge of the table.

ELAINA

Nicholas, I have to talk to you. You are a big boy. I want you to understand what I have to say to you.

(in a lower voice)

I hope you understand.

Mommy has to go. I have to go.

Please, I have to go, Nicholas. Please don't cry. Do not make it harder for me, please. I have to go.

(she is pleading with him)

Surprisingly, Little Nicholas seems to understand.

LITTLE NICHOLAS

(looks at his mother, calmly and thoughtfully for a child of his age)

Okay.

ELAINA

Thank you.

She gets up slowly, goes to the other room, and puts on her acrobatic costume.

She calls Little Nicholas to come into the room with her and sit next to her by the dressing table.

She tries to keep him busy.

ELAINA

Help me, Baby. Give me my makeup and my brush.

Little Nicholas looks around, picks up the right stuff, and hands it to her.

ELAINA

Bravo! Bravo!

(she applauds him then)

My blue eye cream...Smart boy. Smart boy.

(she kisses him)

LITTLE NICHOLAS

I'm a good helper.

(he smiles with satisfaction)

She is almost done. She looks at the clock. It is a quarter to four.

Elaina puts the final touches on her face, standing up in a hurry.

ELAINA

(in front of the mirror)

It is time for me to go.

(she hugs her son and kisses him)

Remember, Mommy loves you very much. Whatever happens, I will always be with you. Remember that.

LITTLE NICHOLAS

I love you too, Mother. Love you too.

(he hugs her for a while)

She gently puts him down.

She kneels in front of her icon and prays. She gets up with tears in her eyes. She takes a couple of steps backward and makes the sign of the cross.

ELAINA

I will see you soon. Okay? Say yes.

(she begs him)

Say yes, please...

LITTLE NICHOLAS

(cracks a smile)

Okay.

Elaina gives him a thumbs, and he does the same.

Elaina pats his head, gives him a kiss, and leaves.

She goes to the circus tent and enters from backstage.

The other performers look at her with surprise and do not say a word.

Pierre is sitting on a bench by himself. He stands silently up as he sees her walking toward him. Elaina stands next to Pierre.

A little girl, who saw Elaina, runs out to the center of the stage while Big Daddy is making his announcements and pulls on the edge of his jacket.

BIG DADDY

What is it? What do you want?

(he stops momentarily and leans down to hear what the little girl is saying)

LITTLE GIRL

(whispers into his ear and leaves)

Elaina is here and is getting ready for her act with Pierre.

Big Daddy looks surprised and relieved. He looks toward the backstage and starts introducing the fantastic acrobatic act...

Applause, but also some boos, are heard from the audience as Pierre and Elaina start climbing their ropes to the landing platform at a steady pace.

They start their performance with their usual act. The audience applauds, and then Big Daddy announces the great attempt.

Big Daddy looks at the space where the net usually hangs. Seeing there is no net, he makes an emotional announcement with his voice breaking.

BIG DADDY

And now, ladies and gentleman, what you are about to witness, is the most dangerous act ever attempted, in the circus world.

What you are going to witness, will be the impossible, Elaina's triple flip in the air, with no safety net bellow

(He chokes, as he tries to go on.)

(In a lowered voice continues)

A failure to succeed. **Will cost, the life, of my most precious daughter Elaina.**

Please, let's have complete silence and pray, for a happy ending.

The crowd gasps when they learn there is no safety net. The circus workers gasp at learning that Elaina is Big Daddy's daughter.

The music starts. Everybody gathers behind Big Daddy, who is anxiously looking up.

Big Daddy is standing at the side of the stage.

Elaina, on her horizontal bar, swings back and forth.

Pierre, hanging with his hands extended, is ready for the crucial moment.

Camera, in slow motion.

Elaina makes her first jump in the air with a good rhythm.

The first flip, followed by a second and then the historical third, is successfully completed.

Pierre's powerful hands made the lifesaving contact, catching her at the right time.

The crowd jumps up, applauding.

PIERRE

(yells loud)

Yes! Yes!

He hands her up to safety on the platform and joins her, giving her hugs and kisses.

A smile of relief fills Elaina's face.

The crowd keeps applauding in a standing ovation, calling bravo! Bravo!

By the time the two of them get down from their platform and walk to the stage, it is full of all kinds of different people (photographers, reporters, performers, and audience members).

Elaina receives a bouquet of flowers from an admirer, and they both receive congratulations, hugs, and handshakes.

BIG DADDY

(looking very emotional, walks by the microphone and announces)

With this historical acrobatic act, ladies and gentlemen, we conclude this afternoon's performance.

Thank you for being here to witness this once-in-a-lifetime accomplishment.

Elaina runs to Big Daddy and hugs him. Holding each other, they walk backstage, where a celebration has already started.

Bottles of champagne pop open, and shots of whiskey are distributed. It's a big party as more and more people keep joining them.

Elaina, all smiles and full of kindness, is thanking everybody.

After a while, she is able to sneak out and run to her trailer.

ELAINA

(in a happy voice, she yells)

I'm back! I'm back!

LITTLE NICHOLAS

Hurray, hurray!

Waiting for his mom, Little Nicholas jumps up from his bed into her arms. They both cry from happiness. They hug and kiss.

ELAINA

I told you I'd be back! I did! I told you... Come on, Little Nicholas, let's get dressed. We are going to have our own party.

She begins wiping her makeup off in a hurry and changes her clothes. Then she helps Little Nicholas get dressed.

She picks up two suitcases from the closet, puts them on the bed, opens them, and throws in some of their belongings. She puts her icon and their pictures on top.

ELAINA

(to Little Nicholas)

You and I are going for a long ride right now!

They walk out of the trailer toward their station wagon, which is parked in front of their trailer.

Elaina is carrying the two suitcases, and Little Nicholas is following, hugging his teddy bear.

She opens the door of the station wagon and places the suitcases in the back. Then she opens the side door and secures Little Nicholas in his car seat.

As she is walking around the car to the driver's seat, she spots Pierre coming out of the back door of the tent. He is holding in his hand an open bottle of champagne, walking very unbalanced, drunk from the glory and the liquor.

He walks toward Elaina.

PIERRE

(very loudly)

We are famous now. We are the greatest!

The whole world will hear about us!

We are famous!

He picks up Elaina and swings her around like a little child. He puts her down.

He holds both of his arms up in the air, and the champagne runs down his hair, face, and clothes while he keeps repeating.

PIERRE

I am the greatest. I did it.

While leaning on the side of the car as Elaina is entering the driver's side, Pierre notices the two suitcases.

PIERRE

Hey, there! Where are you two guys going?

ELAINA

(closes and locks her car door; safe inside, she rolls down the window halfway and answers in a serious voice as she starts the car)

We are leaving. Pierre, we are going away.

PIERRE

(coming over to her window)

You can't do that. You cannot leave now. We are famous. You hear, we are famous!

ELAINA

(putting the car in the driving gear)

Oh yes! Sorry, Pierre, you got the glory that you wanted so badly, but I have a son! I have a son to live for and worry about.

My son needs me alive. Goodbye!

The car slowly drives away.

Pierre follows for a few seconds, and as she pulls farther away.

PIERRE

(screaming)

Stop! Stop!

(sees there is no hope that she is going to stop)

You will be back! You will be back!

ELAINA

(to herself, softly)

Don't bet on that!

She looks at Little Nicholas and cracks a huge smile. So Little Nicholas grins, too. She pats his head and ruffles his hair.

ELAINA

Give me five, Nicholas!

LITTLE NICHOLAS

(ecstatic)

Yup, Mom. Give me five!

They both give the five sign.

They are both smiling and excited.

ELAINA

Let's go home now! We are going home!

LITTLE NICHOLAS

(with enthusiasm)

Yes! Let's go home, Mom!

They drive away on the same road where she and her true love, Nicholas, drove for the first time. Trees on each side of the road and beautiful blue wild flowers are in bloom, as if they are happy for them and wishing them both the best!

EXT. LAKE - MORNING

Mother and son are walking on the pier.

A thick mist covers the lake. At the end of the pier, Elaina sits with her feet hanging down, splashing the water like she did in the old days.

Silhouettes of boats suddenly appear, cutting through the thick mist.

Little Nicholas, standing up next to her, waves to the people on the boats. There are several of them going by with passengers who are talking loudly. Some wave back to him.

There are all kinds of boats: small, large, motor, and sail boats.

Each of the silhouettes, as they pass by little by little, begin to fade away slowly into the thick mist.

Between the silhouettes, a white sailboat appears, as if it is floating above the water, sailing smoothly.

At the steering wheel, standing up, Nicholas' silhouette appears, waving at them.

NICHOLAS

(he waves, calling)

Elaina, Elaina! Elaina, Elaina! Elaina!

ELAINA

(amazed)

Nicholas!

(she whispers and waves back)

Nicholas!

(she replies as tears roll down her face)

(she waves back)

(she waves more and more) (she stands up)

(she waves)

ELAINA

(anxiously)

Nicholas. Nicholas. Nicholas. Nicholas. Nicholas.

(she turns to Little Nicholas)

Wave to your Daddy, Nicholas!

Wave to your Dad.

They both keep waving at the *Breeze of Love* passes by and fades away in the mist of the lake.

The song "Breeze of Love" is heard as the boat slowly disappears.

SONG

"Breeze of Love"

It's that gentle,
lovely touch.
From you, my love,
that I have missed so much.

Like a gentle breeze,
you came into my life.
And you left so soon,
into the morning's light.

This lovely breeze.
This gentle breeze.
Will sail me close to you
someday.

Don't know where.
Somewhere up there.
Our breeze of love.
Will bring me back to you
my love.

Will bring me back to you.

THE END!

Milton Keynes UK
Ingram Content Group UK Ltd.
UKHW022348220124
436511UK00006B/276